Cutting The Cord

Stephen Smith

ORACLE BOOKART PUBLISHING

COPYRIGHT

Cover Art ~ Rein G. @reindrawthings
Interior Art ~ Fatima @fatimasechar
Formatted by ~ Oracle BookArt & PA Services LLC
Printed in the United States of America

CONTENTS

PANDORA'S BOX

"This is the road to love!" the cherubim around me exclaimed. I looked around to find fields of swaying red and pink roses. I was walking along a scarlet brick path. Butterflies, with pearls for eyes, fluttered by. And after a short walk, I came upon a grand building—a masquerade theatre adorned with soft red and bubblegum brick. Marble columns and a gold-laced balcony all around, set in a field of memorable poppies and oregano. I sighed, knowing I had arrived at The Scarlet Heart, yet this was not my destination. Not yet.

A deep breath found me, and I exhaled, hand over heart, what was left of it at least. Like a blood-soaked wedding band, removing my hand was a gifted artifact, an item of power. It was not precisely the flower-of-an-hour I had hoped for, prayed for. I was much too washed up on the Night's Plutonian shore. I took the soft green stem between my shaking fingers as the hand of an angel alighted on my shoulder. Another deep breath filled me as I peered into this blue bud of potential. It remains closed but begins to glow. My body paralyzes as my spirit catalyzes, taking transport to places deeper within.

"This place is a mess," I cry out, standing up from the great fall I thought would have been less. I felt like a half-spilled cup. "I've spent time for more, received less." I looked around at the dilapidated palace.

"You filled it with waters of malice, an underworld of Alice," a voice called out as her figure appeared. A rendering unfeared, adorned in navy blue, gold filling her cracked face hue.

"Good to see you, Memoria," I hugged her. "I don't even think a space rock would cause this much of a messy stir. Then again, my palace is ruin and brr."

I look around. "Remind me, M, to redo this place; it's a mess and needs some silk and lace. Everything is everywhere, like a tangled mess of hair." Pillars, chipped as if attacked by moth millers, dotted everywhere. A towering, shattered case of glass stairs. Walls in shambles, sharp pieces like thorns of brambles. Towers were in rambles.

"Healing is messy," M tells me. "As you heal, so will this place hand in hand. Your valley of ashes, crystalline tears on your lashes. And here they lay hyphenated dashes."

"My broken dreams, torn sashes: marine biologist, zoologist, botanist and agronomist, mime and veterinarian, a good-hearted humanitarian."

"Thought is powerful, as is the mind. It's either a prime component or a rotten rind," Memoria tells me.

We walked to the Pool of Direction, The Original Basin. Four vases are holding my internal water: every mood and emotion, addiction to the commotion. This Basin of Water fed my universe, a collection of planes. Each broke into pieces; each vase poured into each lease. Every single one held its ecosystem. Only flora and fractional insect fauna existed, endemics to each habitat, unique, based upon earthly isms.

The first to the North was the Plane of Eupraxia, an eternal spring and summer. There was no sadness, no emotional bummer. It was joyful, golden sunlight and green fields of many stunning flora. Thalia Moor was where good cheer opened the door. Euphrosyne River fed the plane, feeding the joyful and mirthful rain. Eudaimonia Valley encompassed nearly all, where blessedness did fall. Hedone Hills flourished with pleasure and delight, with all of Eupraxia's flora a welcomed sight.

To the West was the Plane of Shadows. The darkness, the grimness, and the fearfulness resided. Secrets, horrors, skeletons, and ghosts all found their home here, to be wrought once more. Aidos Crater made those feel ashamed and lame. Lyssa Gorge was like rabies; it fed a mad frenzy and rage. Nothing could resolve it, not even white sage. Ate River fed most of the waters here, rippling mischief and infatuation and bringing all to ruin, whereas Eris Hills was where discord did spill. Achlys was Ate's Delta, soaked in sadness and misery. Eleos Fields, a vast, pitiful land of various flora, usually poppies, was fed by the often-flooding waters of Apate Creek, pure waters of fraud, deceit, and deception-drenched recollection.

To the south was the Plane of Emotion, a liquid work shaped by the flowing feeling. River Bia came right through, a flowage of raw energy and potential. Sympathy Valley resided here, as did Sadness Delta at the edge of Bia. Jealously Fault cracked the plane's center, and on the right side was Anger Island. Contrary to the left was the continental shelf of Love, an almost archipelago that many felt but truly did not know. Water-loving flora thrived here, with others being gentle or sheer.

To the East was the Plane of Mindfulness. Tranquility was the oxygen here, with peace and present reigning supreme. The Garden of Pasithea resided here, amongst Lethe Creek, Sophrosyne Lake, Homonia Hill, Alesso Gorge, Iaso Canyon, and Mount Hesychia. Medicinal herbs grew tall and strong within the gorge and canyon like the banyan tree. Oneness was here and union with self. All floral inhabitants were healers and health dealers.

"We have much to do, sir," M picks up a brick.

"That we do, that we do," I kick another with my shoe.

That large blue bud filled with potential, layers of petals sequential. It lay in my open palm again, taken from my choppy heart. A futuristic balance of all chakras, of all my parts. It slowly opens, revealing a golden center of anthers. Pollen tickles my nose as I smell, falling into a mystical well. As I tumbled down and down like Alice, I landed in a large room. Divided yet roomless. A mind palace crafted in partial solace, splattered with stains-white sap rafter rains, walls tall. Plastered in pen, plastered ink papers.

Dead center, seated among a darkened table, a box of splinters. Mahogany wooden. Stylized tattoos. Symbols of the blackbirds of Woden. A pale hand slivers from the shadows. One on the box. The other stops my flesh as she steps into moon-eclipsed light.

A woman so perfect, she is a sin. Pandora, Gardenia. Fallen Angels. Tainted Garden sins. "Open boxes, closed closets, say the same thing; they seek a harmonious ring," Pandora tells me, taking my hand as her image flickers. Box snickers gave way to a red nightgown dressed in form, curled hair, the one and only Gardenia.

"Are you ready?"

"Yes, with Death's hourglass, Time, and its sand," I reply. We reached towards the box, which, in my view, I see wasn't all hers. Carved on its cover were golden letters bearing my name. Our hands hovered over it, and as they touched it, chills went through me.

The lid opened from our aspen grip. "Do not be afraid," Gardenia lays her gold bracelet hand upon my shoulder as whispers echo from the box.

"I am," my words stumble.

"Okay."

The box rumbles.

"A skeleton key to the Great Wall we built," Gardenia sings.

"A grand divide to protect all inside," I say. "To separate us from the pain and keep shadows locked away."

Creaking and reeking, for I was seeking healing, I watched Darkness- organized and Chaos - pour from the black hole that was the box's center. With a dim white, fluorescent glow, slithering streams merged with shadows of mine. Now, one stood before me.

A hairless woman with a navy-blue face with golden cracks like Japanese pottery adorned in a steampunk robe with large buttons and cuffs. "I am Memoria Trust," she says. "Your librarian, to prevent further destruction, detrimental destruction. Because you already have the scars of tomorrow."

"A most honorable librarian," I shake her gold-gloved hand as two ravens alighted upon each shoulder.

"I am Thought," the left squawked.

"I am Memory," the right squawked as they bowed heads to me.

"Your reunion has been waiting, patiently debating. So, let us begin," Memoria motions her hand.

A young child was next. Half a face, half nothingness. Just blank. I knew he was me, clueless and innocent. Seeking morning dew. A lost boy. Withheld. Overprotected. Curious and perplexed. Stained. Traumatized. Shy. It is easy to make cry. Saying he was okay, which was just a lie.

Insecurity came dressed as a jester, purely mocking all it embodied. Dozens of broken horned-mouthed skulls fluttered about it. Each was a different thought- of wrought and woe, insisting I wasn't good enough. My face was ugly, like a troll's. My haircut was a bowl.

"How could someone love this soul?" It mocked.

"You are stolen," a head exclaimed.

"Overweight," said another.

"You are alone, no sister or brother."

Taken back was I, yet my head nodded to it, knowing those were the wrong seeds to sow.

Desire was not an Aphrodite vision, yet it precisely matched the ideas. Half and half -both feminine and masculine. A pink rose petal dress met a red suit below a middle-ground voice that spoke perfectly soft. Perfectly telling me nothing mattered more than the birds and bees. Mother Nature's game logic was lame.

"It only matters what the heart and parts want."

Solitude swirled in, a mere floating spine, forked tail wearing a half-skull mask. Glowing white eyes, small doll-like hands clawed, stroking its stringy hair as I felt all the lonesomeness within its glare. I felt utterly alone. How this constantly gnawed at me. Down to the bone.

Anxiety was next. Anxiousness was its left. Fear was it was right, all on the same face. A black and another white horn shaped the face of this devilish imp. One born of a twisted figure.

"Corrupter of thoughts," I say.

"Bringer of madness. Consumer of Thought. The affliction which spends more than can be bought. You are all the ghosts. All the ghost's ember wrought."

Depression, adorned in a black gown. Those coal-colored robes splintered at their ends with wicked black, red, or white-eyed devils whispering thoughts best left unsaid. Abusers of the head, as it dragged itself in all sloth. Pure but anti-goth, towards me. Devoid of hope.

Deceit, I could not tell from its rose glass veil what gender it was. I could only see the reflective glasses it wore changing the score, blurring reality. Illusions and perfect pictures. Prime suitable sutures trying to solidify my future. Those were not who they seemed. Even their eyes so politely gleamed.

Hope, half man, half woman. Businessman left, flapper right. A flashback memory of them glowing green in the night."

"A little of us goes a long way," he says.

"Do not reside in the past. It should not last and last," she responds.

"Be realistic. Not too much of us. For we are a powerful light," they both say in unison. "No matter the blight."

Anger- a red glow suited in cursed crimson, drinking from a scarlet cup. Holding a carmine pot, sipping on a rage full brew. For his cayenne pepper stew, the more he steamed, the more the pot brewed. It was a sticky, bloody green glue. He was boiling my blood, magma water. All the anger from within.

"What others have done to you," he rasps. "Familial lies, false friendship highs. Those only wanting your thighs."

"Solitude sighs; bald fists can only hit. But with you... I can and will sit."

Jealously was a rag doll-fevered dream in a well of wishes, enchanted by Insecurity when looking at others. "Fathers and mothers, sisters and brothers want to be rich, not poor. Wanting facts, not lore. Not wanting to be alone, seeing all the couples sewing false rhymes. Wishing to be others was my heart's worst crime".

Guilt was strewn in purple, sopping wet with despair, truth or dare. Voodoo doll hair and fury like a bear. There was no care, no matter, just streams of regret that met the seven sins. Cycle after cycle, it happened again, forming a bottomless pit until I learned to let go.

The jumbled figure, stumbling and tattered with bruises, looked at me. I knew it: Abuse, Misuse holding a corncob pipe. White powder mustache, cigarette bracelet, nicotine necklace, poppy pod pendant, and amphetamine breath. Those black and blue bruises on his face, scars on his heart, and blood-tipped fingers. He'd been through the wringer, held by Desire's Brother-Temptation.

Desire handed me a stained glass, broken heart. It shattered and became two twins: Hurt and Pain. "I took residence at the intersection of Fifth and myself," said Hurt, "where you nor I stray too far from the sidewalk. So, we don't end up lined in chalk, missing our heart."

Pain took Hurt's shaking hand. "Playing on the safe side so we don't feel Hurt. To keep our heart from misery, since it adores company, to not fall so hard. All these people made it hard to trust yourself and everyone around you." He squeezes Hurt's hand.

"And you let everyone around you, The Thieves, into your head. In your bed. That great divide, so you'd never fall so hard again. So, no one, not even yourself, could win. It was brick by brick, stone, mud, words, and sticks. It blacked out the brilliant sun that precious light growing so tall. And in the end, what did you make?"

I sighed. "Bullets to a broken gun."

~opening of pandora's box

I was in a nightmare. A haunted dream. Cradling my box. Feeling as if I was standing upon jagged, molten rocks. In front of me, it stood. They stood. A two-faced creature. Half demon, half preacher. Under one arm, a blue book of leather, bound by the golden threads of the Past feather. A blank title page, barren, like its cover.

"I am Suspicion," It points a finger at me. "I am your teacher. If you pull, I push too deep. A chase is barren and Relentless. Exhausting and senseless."

"Faded stars, dead fireflies in jars. Taking things out of context. Telling yourself..."

"I bet," I nod.

"I think."

"I should have."

"I could have."

"A grizzly ghoul, but you're doing better," said Memoria.

"Improvement!" squeaked Thought.

"You cried in the night for Pain, screamed for Anger and Hurt. Feared Fear, change," squealed Memory. "Suspicion is always your shadow."

"Trust taught me boundaries. Their value and safety within them. Don't let everyone in. Be cautious, but not too cautious."

"Anxiety taught fear, their power, and how they can shape me and reality. It showed me areas needing strength and others where I should let go. Fear is normal; just don't let it become you."

Depression taught me that the environment, who, and what you're around drastically affected you. It can even become you."

"Look inward into the darkness," Memoria breathes, "and find the light. Seek help when needed, even if

Solitude taught me that alone is okay. It leads to growth and discovery. In small doses properly placed with those we love, it is recovery."

~boxed in lessons

A large door appeared, ebony black. A drab skeletal figure guarded it as I walked past and entered a grand hall. Dozens of doors and solid white floors followed a glowing light into which I stepped. Coming out, it was into a valley. A paradise with fields that are ever-green and rolling. Impish figures were fluttering and strolling, hills rolling. Flowers abloom.

I stood at the base of a grand wood. Memoria to my left, with birds on my shoulder. Suspicion on my right, a heavy-weight boulder. Running my fingers across its cosmic bark, finding runes carved as tales of time.

The whistling startled me. Suspicion tensed as we looked up, gaining a viewpoint sense of the shooting star. A falling orb close but from afar, landing in front of us, in front of me. It was then I could see. What stood before me. Who stood before me.

She, a most beautiful feminine, carried a silver measuring rod and pink lilies in a basket adorned in a simple white gown and red-brown Icho gaeshi hair held by gold pins. So jolly was she as she skipped to me, sprinkling yellow dust from the lilies as she went sprouting flowers upon flowers, stopping and holding out her arms as I smiled and embraced her gentle hugging caress.

"So good to see you," she softly says, wiping the tears from my eyes. "And your guests." Trust bowed, as did Suspicion.

"Oh, Sister," she sang gently, swaying side to side like a sunflower. "We have a visitor."

"Oh yes, Sister," a voice calls out from beneath the large root. "I've been here. Tending this Mister." The clicking of a wooden door gives way to Her figure, adorned in a gold-edged white medieval bodice bottomed with a simple white gown like her sister, covered in flowers and a sprig of myrtle in her gold pinned red-brown, Momo ware hair.

Trickling off her in blue, green, and white hues, swirling and dancing. Her spindle, a paintbrush, and potential colors every move she made cascaded kept images of the past. Deer running, Australopithecus, Homo erectus families, Passenger pigeons, Carolina parakeets, Tasmanian tigers, Big Bang collisions and gases, the birth of every solar system. DNA helixes, RNA dust devils, the evolution of man, ice ages, the sinking of the Titanic, the Salem witch trials and panic, Darwin's landing of the Galapagos, the invention of the telephone, wheat, and maize domestication. Cleopatra and Ramses' rule, signing of the Declaration, passing of the Magna Carta, Beowulf, the first emperor of China, Indigenous People on horseback, and a mustached dragon that landed back in her hair.

"The Past in all its radiant glory," she stands before me as I bow.

"No need to bow," she says. "While I am royalty, the gesture is of old days, as is your soul. But yes," a squirrel runs up her gown and sits on her shoulder, munching a large berry. "I am the Past's glory, a collection of everyone's trauma and drama. Partly the reason you are here, my earthly dear."

Suspicion hands me the book out of its many arms. The cover shifts, carrying the seven stages of man, stages of I; from birth to the time to die.

"It needs to be bleached," she could read the whys slivering from my eyes. "You're ready," she says, taking the book. "Let us take a look at your collection of The Past. The Beginning, yet The Last. First, we shall cast," she caresses the book. "Keepings of Memory, no pages broken. Reveal thy selves, show the spoken word tokens."

Her powerful fingers graced my spine, my shivering, my body quivering. Her gentle touch ethereally ripped and unlaced the bindings. "Let us look at what is after, what came from broken rafters, from the unraveling of us."

~present reflections

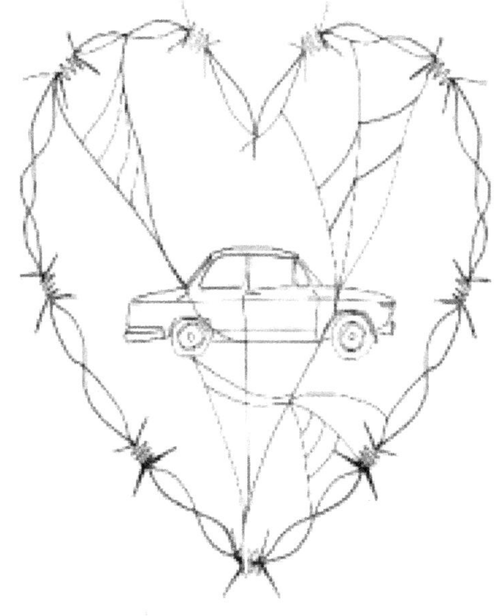

MERCURY RETROGRADE

"I've been a fool," I said.
"Yes, you have," you replied. "But you're my fool."

~confess to me

Impulses. Visions from the past. Craving what was once had. Doing everything, but forgetting you.

~this is the end

all i ever wanted
on these clouds of recollection
was your devotion
not a concoction
a pandora's box decoction
you were a false
false anti-toxin
~choking on you

looking at it all now
we were a storm on the beach
power out
everything wrong
but feeling alright
~hailstones

i used to tell myself
i shouldn't have let you drift away
i shouldn't have let it all end
that no one else what we did
and that was only because
i didn't know i deserved better
~regret talking

I tried not to feel it. I tried not to need it.
I tried not to require you. But I couldn't.
I couldn't stop thinking about you.
~holy fool

I am trying not to want you. I am trying not to miss you. But it's not going well. Do you ever think of me? Am I more than a flicker in your head? A space in your bed?

~out on this lonely road

A freshly weeded garden was I. Rain fell again, and I cried. Dormant seeds sprouted, and I drowned in you once again. No matter how hard I tried, you always won. Backward motion. Resurrected emotion. Internal commotion.

~stuck in my mind

i was a firewalker
stepping on your hot coals
i was a firefighter
shield less in a burning house
my tears
my cries
just drama in a silent picture
~aftertaste

when i was young
so captivated and foolish
i thought the world of you
you were all i wanted
until it faded
and i saw i'd never see you again
~un-desire

i found faux beauty
in your east egg green light
living in that shadow
of hopeless light
~i lie flat in west egg

The clouds seemed to draw you in like the scent of fresh rain. A tidal wave of pain. Back again, am I questioning whether we were both sane? You were a god to me. So strong. So free.

~scars on my mind

You left on a Wednesday. "I'll call you on Monday," you told me. I was then caught up in your game. That was the last I heard. Your leaving, your expulsion, only shaped me for the worst. It turned my cityscape into dust.

~where am i?

My first love was ripped away from me. The secrets I learned never did free me. The ex-lovers have far too vibrant memories—resurrected agonies. The swamp water is so stale. It was Grendel stuffed into a well.

~grendel's marsh

The troll was the only thing left under the bridge after it burnt and exploded. That monster of us. It grew so cold, as I did. Our garden was now a barren wilderness; the only warmth and comfort I had left was that troll.

~damage done

the glistening flames
what we once were
arise
even flicker
out of smoldering coals
deadly desires
for which i got burnt
~even fireflies die

i came to realize
like soaking creosote
you weren't the oar
to steer my boat
you were a roller coaster
a haunted sort
you were a bathtub toaster
an electrical ride taking me up
crashing me down
giving false butterflies
~glasswing

i think we do it
without much thought
giving ourselves away
that's what i did
and kept giving myself away
rotting my garden
souring my green pastures
because i was giving myself away
to past lovers
~finger on self-destruct

every time i saw you
i ran over and over
scurried like a nuclear rover
each time now
i see what a four leaf wasn't clover
~confessions

we were glass breaking
didn't belong together
no grand masterpiece
tragedy awaited us
but i wrote us as godly
~couldn't escape us

it was just a dream
they were dreams
a set of fevered reams
sewing and recutting seams
of mere dreams
~i can't even sleep

swam in shiny pools
rolling golden thread onto spools
life oh so swell
but i tumbled
forcibly fell
cause what i thought i wanted
let me down
~could i escape you

i gave you my heart
i was a fragile boy
a white lily
you let go to waste
the blood spilly
you left
and i was just silly
~madness of you

you fed me a poisoned apple
i fed myself tainted wine
silver chalice
golden goblet
midnight crawling
i a pile of feathers
broken starlin'
~hiding is dishonest

i'm a walking contradiction
a mask of affliction
self-created conviction
running when the sun goes down
wearing red flag warnings
~theatre drama

my shadow
my own being
a crazy angel
tilted halo
foggy shine
flies low tonight
~fallen angel

a storm rolling in
maybe its rain will put out this wildfire
started years ago by your lighter
an overgrown canopy
hell-bent on sunshine
~strangler figs

rolled ups and moonshine
fox grapes on the vine
thought surfacing
hell bent on moonlight
because i was a lunatic
a loose end
caught in a landslide of you
~landslide of you

i was a well kept child
curious but not wild
the forest
the trees
the animals
all didn't come out
until the past
i began logging
~waves of letting go

i became a reckless wild
dead end mile
living on the run
parallel to Blanche's tracks
a lost soul
a twisted road
~streetcar tracks burn red

i was a hopeless romantic
trust lacking frantic
pandemonium panic
a heartfelt desperado
a shot in the dark
without hope
~masquerade master

you changed my universe
rewrote my galaxy
painted new scars in my night sky
a green path
on the barren wayside
everything i lost
you found
treasure hunter
el dorado bound
~gold is worth millions

every day once seemed
a story book over and over
the same
no sun
pouring rain
incinerated martian rover
feeling so alone
~i'm stuck here existing

you gotta do what you gotta
moving through you
moving on
i got one step forwards
my other stuck in the past
holding on
~remove the glue of you

the talk of those apple trees
the cherries
the walnuts
they remind me of you
of what was good back then
you were young
i was something
chasing lightning
~tainted fruit

at the time i didn't know
know what i'd lose
never thought it'd be me
never thought it'd be you
~mindless

before i entered the
battlefield
my shield glowed
my spears and swords dull
non-existent
~courageous soldier

thought we were on better days
yet boarded a jack knifed freight train
no brakes
no stops in the future
~train bent on no where

i let them go
i left them in the cold
everything so heavy
leading myself on
let myself go
without second thought
~plowing through

i couldn't stand the thought
the thought of goodbye
of a real leaving
one you promised me
that it wouldn't be
the world got colder
you quit looking for me over
over your shoulder
and i never really got closure
~midnights became afternoon

i took a rocky path
been down broken road
this is where it ends
i'm breaking down
cause you lied
that things would work out
~path of our end

you promised me the moon
sitting under the stars
yet that first flame blew out
a criss-cross wind
i don't know id it'll get relit
as i fade into the sunset
trying to forget
~stacked rocks in the mist

i was broken
you long gone
it all went wrong
wrote heartbreak songs
tried to hold on
yet you still
still slipped from my fingertips
~holding so strong

i hate my heart sometimes
as i hide under the covers
scared of the dark
~little child fears

blame it on your mom
blame it on your dad
die young
live fast
is that the only remedy?
the only remedy for us
the remedy for everything
~is this true

i await
your arrival
a grand bird of paradise gesture
lighting of the rusted neon
that burnt out sign
in my chest
a hollowed out vacancy
a flicker of light
you left
~hotel heart shutdown

a heart shaped hole inside
filling with anything
burning bridges and forests
crossing muddy roads
of those who could guide me
ego got the best of me
became the worst of me
until i made
took a slice
of humble pie
~humble pie

i wielded insecurities
tears falling on blanche's seats
a taste of regret
what is real
only pain i feel
~red leather seats

felt no connection
felt no direction
no searching
only a breaching
of your memory
~you're all i see

there's a time i remember
when pain was unknown
no bloody cans
to graffiti my heart
when i believed forever
where there was no change
and my heart was in spring
not december
~fresh white paint

for so long i've waited
i still wait
atop a grassy knoll
a wait so long
that i almost entered biological stasis
dormancy in oasis
feeling fit for no one
until that dream
of you
~help me hypnos

coiled up
like a venomous serpent
you
fruit of temptation
as i'm tangled in your trance
your hooks in me
giving me
that endangered chance
~you, of good and evil

i had a river running to you
from waterfalls
that were my eyes
a blood trail
from your bullets and knives
reds mixed with blues
all shades
all hues
all you
~i keep seeing water

oh love
false love
i mistaken you for a sign
a sign from above
~we were false

ive been broken into fractions
memories
like photochemical reactions
words like contractions
and you were a false divine distraction
~heaven can't help me now

i woke up surrounded
a haze of frozen planets
icy shards
orbiting the vacuum
you became
~big bang two

i wrote them
created them
yet even some turned on me
surrounded me
talking to me
damage
consequence
~words became real

bury me within this bed
you're stuck in my head
labyrinth bed
time is dilated
like we spent
fascinating
threading a needle
over
and over
again
~can't help i need you

its cruel
the memories
the blue of your eyes
like blasphemy
making even angels cry
cause when i was with you
it was nothing else
now i see
it gave me welts
~fever blister

dawn gives me aches
dusk makes me long
five years and you still haven't gone
parts of me
cracks and crevices
still hold on
~you put out my flame

i wasn't ready
even though you made my heart
my mind
unsteady
how easy you'd replace me
how easy you'd forget me
~insincere balance

i told you
i frown
unhealthy
is all i know
~once truth

i think id rather hear your regrets
your original sin
about me
than deal with this
memory
~holding up my heart and head

daylight quake
night ache
my heart still at your place
feeling the same
cause there are scars
uneasy to erase
~good with over thinking

understanding fuzzy
clarity wuzzy
couldn't explain
until the realization
we fall for familiar pain
~our familiarity

maybe i was a fool
for falling for you
thinking i loved you
letting you in my bones
when i had nothing to lose
~fallen out of love

nothing more to give
at least for that short time
i did live
our ship went down
i almost buried myself
almost
to drown
~hit the iceberg called us

we lied an inch apart
we lied inches apart
extinguished stars from start
on your own continuum
truth and passion
a minimum
~beautiful mistake

i was kept from setting sail
in many different ways
i lost much of the love i held
lost myself
sinking beneath it all
weighed down with a wall
where i searched
where i reached
on faith
in false rivers
for you
~lost on you

i went to anger
i lept into the danger
my eyes like fire
ego a winged insect
i on a viking ship fire
i bit through their wire
a waking hell
waking healing
as my wicked gods
grow tired
~inner war

for the time being
for a while
i avoided my own questions
buried our deep history
world war trenches
trying to hold you in my breath
forever
~things, those secrets

you are a perfect reminder
all these scars on my mind
all these wounds in my heart
of if i can hold myself
together
~blade of a letter opener

i choked on
waiting
basking in solace
souring in regret
~defibrillator dance

you guided me
i beckoned the rivers
begged the tides
to carry you back to me
wash me upon your shores
~shore of you

no amount
no self sought fury
black soil to bury
could bring back
return to me
past glory
that innocence
~lost in the garden

guess its all too late now
we'll never know
that's how it was meant to go
before i had that fall
tumble from Eden
onto a lonesome road
no right way
for my heart
for my mind
to go
~midnight train

you were a raging storm
unclear thoughts
a dirtied mind
the future got unclear
but you turned see through
a i knew then
i didn't know you
~dirty pout

my rooster crowed at dawn
yours crowed at dusk
i drifted away
like a dusty rose
fell asleep
an opium drip
~morphine iv

every time so far
up to now
i've never heard it
not in it's purity
even when it was the two of us
that i
i was everything you've always
wanted
~don't want you

stuck in space
wrapped in rhyme
living a lonely life
entombed by time
trying to survive
walking down a blank road
not knowing
where it even goes
~it took one to end me

you illuminate me
bioluminescence
you dream of me
phosphoresce
you care for me
acquiescence
you are true emotion
incandescence
you warm me
thermoluminescence
my dreams
fluorescence
you
omnipresence
bleeding through spaces
you're drifting in the fog
i didn't know where to go
and couldn't divide
the crystal waters
~mind in a freefall

We jumped from crumbling bridges, tossing ourselves from burning buildings," Blanche sang. "Surrounded by letters from a dead boy. Kisses on the necks, forehead pecks, from the lovers once held in our arms."

I take her hand, joining her longing gaze on stage. "They stepped onto the papers, snatched them from our very hands," I sang. "The crumbling was a rumbling, their words a stumbling. A search for more humbling, a strong IV of numbing."

Her gaze and mine met like salty and freshwater currents. "Our shadows are soaked in fear," we let slip from our eternal lips.

"The grimy teeth, it's black soot. Soot that drags us always foot by foot," I lower my head.

"I am the shadows," she solemnly tells me, a tear streaming down her face so grim. "My lanterns burnt out, permanently dim."

~torturous monsters

My delivery was in a cursed red crimson car. A chauffeur from a chained heart bar; gasoline fuel the craving of the past. And I lost myself. I lost myself that day you walked out the door, states away. Nothing helped, not even to pray. I thought I would love you until the end of time. Yet we were a star-crossed rhyme. Soot covered—spoiled grime.

~mercury retrograde

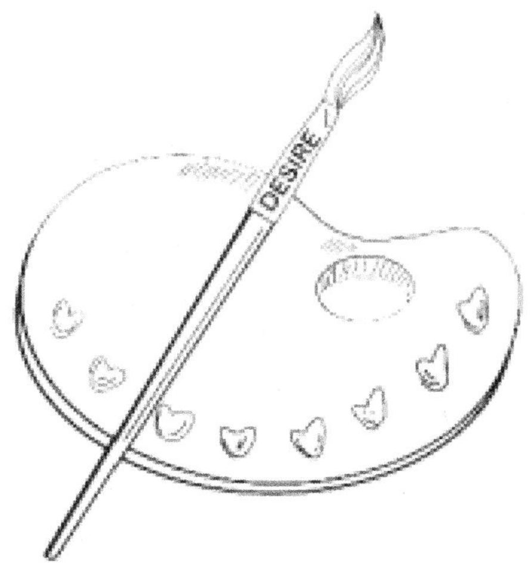

CANVAS OF LOVE

i won't forget
i can't forget
what we shared
first love
first taste
~alone in the garden

put my life on pause
ignored the whys
lost more and more
so i guess
that's the cost of holding onto heartbreak
~holding burnt matches

told me i was crazy
you lost track
words rolled off that silver tongue
just like you
fabricated love
~love by the bottle

I spat blood upon waking up
I screamed terror from your nightmares
Porcelain stained I was
White roses
Black doves
I hope you see what I become
What wasn't love
~tired of missing you

our memories
medusa's glance
sharp as a lance
i
a broken tulip
infected by false
pestilence
as we crumbled
broken porcelain
~white vase with red tulip

Transportation made of cold steel and mercury. Driven by Solitude, The Monaxia steered towards Desire. Brakes squeal, hearts steal, sparks fly. Horns blow, bells ring. It was my arrival at Desire Shoals.

A gathering was going on, a fair. Or more so, an affair. Giant tents arose in the air, each Monax an affliction, this carnival of carnal contradiction. The thoughts were clowns, gypsies, tall men, bearded women. My destination was in the back, behind the Ferris wheel that did shine, behind it all.

I was walking, following a solid red brick road. The Road to Love, littered with petals of rose and fox gloves. Raindrops began to fall, and I could hear the snickering, the call. This rain was a sentimental hall, a tearful waterfall. It soaked the brick, caressed my hair, and in the distance was a flashing glare, that caused me to stare. A flashing sign illuminated high and tall. *Dirty Pout.*

It was a dimly lit room upon my entry into Pout. Divided it was, at least in two. Dim met light as I wandered across the marble floor, inhabited by figures causing de ja vu. Many here reminded me of you.

"What will you have?" a familiar voice asked. I sat on a stool as the bartender turned around, illuminated in neon blue light.

"Desire!" I gasped. "Desire? Desire!"

"Hello, my love," she leans over and hugs me. She smelled jasmine and vanilla as she spun around, twirling the translucent red silk gown amongst a flow of long, curled strawberry blonde hair, at least here in this place of soaked despair. Her eyes met mine, a perfect stare.

" Why a bar?" I look around.

"Why not one?" She smiles. "You've never been a bar type, I know."

"Yet, here we are, Desire," I chuckle. "I'll take a Love is a Lie," I told her, knowing the menu all too well. It was an all too reflective menu, tailored precisely to me.

"Excellent choice," she began mixing, moving like a velveteen Rolls Royce. Lavender incense filled the room, thunder echoed, and lightning flashed, each boom giving a vein-like splash. The void of a roof was now nothing but storm.

Desire stuffed a pink straw in, with a sprig of mint atop the red drink, on ice. I took a sip, smiling with satisfaction. "Delicious as always, my dear." She grins and swirls from behind the bar to the stool beside me.

"An interesting place you built," she says. "Here on your Solo-plane of Love."

"All of my circus performers are in here. It is not entirely how I perceived love; it is a mess, nothing too great, nonetheless. Very reflective, maybe criminally warranting a detective, of my mess." I sip.

"Now, now," she rubs my shoulder. "It is a shoal, a shoal of boulders. It isn't complete. It has suffered neglect, deplete."

"My own deplete. The delete," I sigh. A microphone tap disrupts me, making me turn abruptly to the stage. "What's the entertainment this evening?"

"Who, not what," Desire smiles as the storm cloud curtains, outlined in blue, pulled back.

I had to catch my breath. "Is that...."

"Blanche DuBois? Why, it is!" Desire whispers. I gasped again; my eyes fixated on her. She was daintily dressed in a white suit and a fluffed bodice, hiding like a lit cockatrice. Pearl earrings and necklace, white gloves and hat. It was most certainly a garden district arrival.

"Ravishing, isn't she?" Desire smirks.

"More than I have words for, yes." She began to sing softly but potently. Various poems I had written. Yet one, one stood out like a finely lit boat.

I look to Desire, nodding. She takes my hand as we move to the front. Blanche's voice was in perfect font as we dodged figures. I remained here, captivated for a while. Desire danced softly next to me to music from The Fifth Symphony. Then it broke like a raging fever.

I turned around to the scattered crowd. Blanche's song was still loud. "Let me see your faces!" I cried out, pouting and proud.

"You heard him dearest figures! Dismember, disfigure!" A voice called out.

I twirled back around to the stage. Red and pink mists and incense formed a seashell figure of loving rage. She was radiantly beautiful, divinely. Long, ocean-flowing hair. Fair skin, abalone shell bikini, below a purely translucent gown.

"Aphrodite!" My lips quivered as she joined Blanche. The Fifth Symphony and my ears only rang louder, creating a siren song with Blanche and Aphrodite as they sang.

I turned around again and cried out. White lights shot on. All figures became illuminated as Desire led me to the stage, it's floor fossilized coral.

I stood and stood. I looked; I saw. The cracks, the flaws. They were all here: Eros, Himeros, Anteros, Peitho, Suadela, Atlas, Amor, Harmonia, Priapus, Pan, Hedylogos, Pothos, Hebe, Antheia, Hymenaios, Aglaea, Euphrosyne, Thalia, Diana, Flora, Bacchus, Concordia, Hedone, Charis, Amia, Chrysaor, Pragma, Epithumia, Metanoia and Mania. They all were disguised in various guises of my past love. Each with a drink in hand, and next to them, to all of them, were the specters of myself, the ghosts of those times. The ghosts of me.

Tears welled in my eyes. I could see, I saw, I was never truly alone. I began to speak as Desire refilled my glass. "On the Solitude Train, it's easy to feel that these past relationships, these so-called track records, were my end, my failures. Undatableness."

"Yes, they were failures. False saviors because I couldn't grow. I didn't know. The lessons have been in front of me all along. Don't forget your worth, rescue dating, conversions, and fixings, not doing what I needed for myself. I was a false savior. I don't need to fix; I don't need to earn my place. I value your time and care because I have lived self-sacrifice, giving all of me. Mentally, spiritually, physically, emotionally. This was my concept of love; it was wrong."

"Trust your gut, because not put me in a rut. Don't go in or do if it feels wrong. Ask the hard questions. Don't go second guessing."

"Fulfillment isn't from someone else; it lies within you, within me. Life's fulfillment isn't about one. Someone might help, but it truly comes from within, from other meaningful moments and events. Don't get too invested early on; no texters should set the day to ruin. I should have held a better relationship with myself, a better union. No one has happiness over me except for me."

"I have kept the same choices, the bramble patterns, because of comfort. Because of conformity. That fright of change when there are indeed different lanes. Dwelling on past flaws, digging in of their claws. I have, and they have remained so raw. I picked apart what was wrong, doing that faux dance and song. So much I couldn't establish new, weighing attraction on faults."

"Pain is a necessity for growth, not the ignorance of its existence or removal. The devastation, the pure heartbreak, must be felt and experienced to bring me closer to a more positive future. To myself."

"See the person for the person, for whom they truly are. Take into consideration their past and faults, their defaults. Don't see them as an expectation based upon the past, upon the last. Not as standards low or high. Know and see someone, not by your definition."

"Be yourself, even with small tokens. There is value in patience and small doses. No masks, no suits, as you cannot fake forever. Honor the truth, live it; it is the evidence and proof."

I cried more and more, only truly noticing the sheer number of tears when Desire wiped my eyes. Suddenly, in that moment, the room was brightened by beams of sun. The forms of me were all smiling, some too crying, arms interlaced with all those here. They turned and kissed them, where they rippled and vanished. All the Me's began coming together, absorbing as they formed a single me, holding a red crystalline heart, bearing a few cracks.

Aphrodite and Blanche stopped singing and strutted over to me, taking my hands. "I am proud of you for this," Aphrodite said with a great smile.

"I didn't think I could do it," I responded.

"You did!" Blanche exclaimed. "Please remember those who may have not worked out, those parts of you, those lessons. They were experiences, memorable gestures. They were real people, all in their woes. Some are ice, some are fire."

"Carry these forwards with you," Desire leans onto me. "Don't stop caring about yourself."

"Love yourself," Aphrodite tightens on my hand. "Please do not ever blindly recognize yourself."

"Don't let flaws become truth and reality. Let the past be just that, keeping the lessons in your new hat," Desire seduces. "Be you for you."

I was indebted to them all, but they promised me I owed them nothing. "May I have this dance, dear?" I held my hand to Desire as Aphrodite and Blanche smiled.

"Of course, darling." She takes my hand. We slowly danced as Aphrodite and Blanche sang.

After a while, we stopped, and they hugged me, kissing my cheek. The stage lights dimmed, and Blanche receded into darkness. Desire and Aphrodite all waved goodbyes. I smiled and turned to the guy. He had waited patiently all night, calmly and respectfully through everything. He was I and we hugged in a great embrace. Upon loosening, we headed for the door; I held his hand. Our other two were clutching that ruby red heart."

~conversations with love

i get choked up
breathing hard to do
my mind goes black
my lungs blue
my heart feels
as if it'll break in two
i need a little love
a little love
~recalling all about you

you travelled on
left me behind
that's okay
i was alright
you tried
tried to turn on the lights
those beams i used to leave on
but i found no use
the bulbs burn out
and like you did to me
i left you on the dark side of
the road
~hitchhiker

the past is past
sand in the hourglass
no more between my fingers
no more to last
no use in looking back
i know what i deserve
~spell it out

Flashes of the memories, tears swelling in my lashes, of the battles rattled me as I stood up. They hit me in a blur, every one a single spur.

A scarlet and silver-lettered street sign sparkles in the diluted sun, hidden in a smokey haze. The humidity, the heat, reminded me. Dug into me. I was taken back to August and September.

A figure appeared in the near distance. Shadows are still ever so persistent. Long hair and a gown were flowing. I knew it was Desire. She disappeared, and I whirled around, hearing horse hooves and neighing. My heart was heavy, memory weighing. Out of the haze, in my glistening gaze, rose a chariot. Pure white horses carried it; rose gold, silver etched. Aphrodite holds the reigns. Her passenger was Desire.

Desire stepped down. Adorned in a transparent war gown. Vermillion army boots, black laces, and a cardinal toile-robed business suit.

"I've never seen you in war regalia," I tell her.

She takes off her heart-shaped helmet. "We both know the matters of the heart are the worst form of war."

I nod, my legs and arms feeling like a hot rod. Cherubs were shoveling maroon and fire engines, magenta pebbles, and dust from the hundreds of craters and holes across the land. This wasteland of war. Scars and shattered parts. These were the Carnage Fields.

"You're bleeding, been bleeding." Desire points behind me. Dragging along, like a haunted dress train, was a ruby stain. Splotches and blotches, all in candy apple.

"Blood and red do stain," I sigh. I look up at Desire with eyes holding pain. "What is it, Desire?"

"It's your past talking. It's creeping out from its crypt, stalking." She motions her hand outwards, pink sparkles flying. The wind catches them and her gown, blowing in all directions. Projections They, Them, of the lovers began to appear in the fog and smoke.

Tears soaked my eyes as I began to choke. "The first few times of seeing you and the last are still very much burnt in my mind. Orange is like orange rind. I gave you everything. The roses, you left there to die.

Aphrodite's apparition, shadowy in all the smoke and haze, shuffled around. Her horses, potent stallions, took the shape of humans, coin figurine medallions. Her shapes filled the field as bullets and bombs sailed past me, all heart-shaped grenades.

Algea's voice, all their voices, echoed in every direction. It's a slow-motion love potion.

"Apology after apology, it was almost a eulogy." I walk past a large crater filled with pink dust powder and shattered heart shards. "Summer was so beautiful. I was laughing in the passenger side ride. And I realized I loved you in the fall."

"Your birthday, my birthday, passed, and neither of us called." The memorization became sharp as Aphrodite's voice began to hum and sing out like a thousand angelic harps. Shadows and haze took their shape. Resurrecting from my tombs of silence.

"Street walks, late night talks. Truck bed laying, farm swaying. Dinners and garden work. The windows open, and music blares on Fifth Avenue. Tears were going up the Street of Hurt." I turned to Desire. "Broken promises and tattered stories. It was war; it wasn't fair."

"They were the burnt-out pocketsful of crossed stars. Remnant scars. They were midnight thoughts. Midnight, late night, glooms and shrooms," Desire replied softly, a grenade slamming into the ground behind her.

I stopped as shadows and dust formed the figures of a young, shaggy-haired me running down Fifth Avenue, tears streaming down my face as I lost the gleaming. "Nights where I nearly thought I lost you."

I shook my head, trying to rid myself of the dream, the mirage, the cursed vision. It was like an infected incision. "I could see it was I, and on the charted ground, I did lie. A crimson red World War suit and pink beret. The heart stains looked like red Cabernet. The Cupid Calvary is printed in gold embroidery. He was broken and blue.

"You finally fought back in the strongest way feasible. No longer pleasurable."

"You severed ties, ended the lies. His memory lives on, yes, but it isn't physicality. Only a mentality." Desire watches a cannonball land behind me.

"I was away for so long. Out of touch. A familial sucker punches."

"It wasn't wasted time," Desire says. "I know that's what you think. It isn't tainted, no wretched stink."

"I was figuring things out. Scream and shout. Joy and pour. Weak and stout."

"Precisely," Desire nods. "Finger on hairpin triggers or not. You didn't rot."

"You were you," my lips shiver as I stare at my war-drenched figure. "To me, freedom was nothing but missing them. But it was much more." I reached out my hand as Calvary looked up, still broken and blue. He shakily took my hand as I pulled him up. I saluted him and hugged him. Closing my eyes, he vanished just as he had appeared.

"If you could love them again, go back in time and change it, would you love them better? Is it all right? Love them again?" Aphrodite's voice echoed out.

"No," I say sternly. "It wasn't written in the stars. It would never have worked."

"That is growth, darling!" She cheerfully shouts.

"Look back with acceptance and joy. Calm the darkness," Desire says as she begins walking towards me.

"They still bloom in my memory garden."

"Most first loves to do. Yet, that's all, too. A garden overcome with weeds only instills wicked seeds."

"Look at me." I slowly meet her radiant face as she takes my hands into hers. "It is okay to remember. Summer days may feel like December. Even bitter February. But you control your merry. The pain you let haunt and carry. Don't be weary."

"Remember, just don't stir false embers. Plant a garden if you desire. Don't get caught up in rusty wire." She smiled at me as she took my hand and gently rolled it into a fist, helping me kneel.

My palm lay flat on the soil, and for a moment, the pain jolted through me. Anxiety, fear, memory. A sign appeared carved from mahogany. *Carnage Field*, it read. Heart-shaped vines encased it, blooming in trumpet flowers speckled and spotted. Reds, blues, and pinks were their petals dotted.

Aphrodite's seashell bikini rattled as she swayed over to me." The fields next door, the freshwater shores, all are yours. They are blank pages, untouched by any past ages."

~in the flowers' face is me

take
take away the doubt
take
take away the misuse
take
take away the rust
take
take away the distrust shouts
take
take me for me
~take as you see

i don't want to get in your way
i don't want to scare you away
yet we haven't met
and still i pray
but i think i can after long say
while still healing
ive done done much peeling
relinquished the stealing
my own scammer dealing
became locked away
in a box buried on eupraxia
is that moment
you smiled at me
~breathe life into me

we had a good run
dead end streets
hearts loaded like a gun
stealing down stars
crashing the moon
you loved the wind
once wrote on my page
now its different chapters
and no happily ever after
~willing to walk away

life goes on with or without them
if they're willing to leave
even if it leaves a blood stained sleeve
don't beg them to stay
convince yourself to stay
pain only comes from reminiscing
~pain in those poppy petals

i was a wreck
i was a mess
a toppled over game of chess
getting over you felt wrong i must confess
i now must forget
and forgive myself
~healing love

I was seated yet again, being treated by Desire to another drink at The Pout. What was the Pout? Now, it's The Scarlet Heart. It's not precisely a rename, more so a removal of that shame and blame.

"It's time," I sighed, finally sitting at a place that was not the bar. I was not in a position too far.

I was not entirely alone, as other entities enjoyed the newly renovated, rejuvenated. Eros and Psyche sat in the far corner, bedazzled by each other. Cupid was watching, a table to his own, frazzled. Hurt and Pain were in a booth and for once, smiling over mint cocktails.

"Let Them in," I call out. A Monaxia hurried to the large doors, now no longer grim like the moors, and opened them.

There They came, towards me, a smile on their face. Age had betaken them, yet youth still glowed. Same color hair, same face with added details, same outfit, meant for showy retail.

We hugged and sat down. "We can finally talk," I say, sipping the elderflower gin-o-tonic delivered by Desire. She rubbed my shoulder as she wandered back to the bar, knowingly hitting my shoulder scar.

"I can understand you here," they say, taking a sip of a whiskey neat. "So, please speak freely."

"This place, this world, it was built for many reasons, mainly because of that past dance we did, through every season," I begin. "A star fell from your heart, hovered over my chained shores, landed within the coldness, as you became the light within my eyes."

"I screamed your name, memories, moments, slowly letting go and re-threading our rope. Trying but also falsely untying, unraveling us. You were in my head, and I let myself down," I added, drinking.

"I let you down, too. I stepped all over you, all the promises. Ripped, tore at your heart," They blink, staring at me.

"I heard your heartbeat, felt that relentless heat. Saw your apparition in the dark. You were a stark contrast to what I thought and knew."

"We felt the same," They sigh. "I saw your face in the night sky, in the white lines. The front yard, home steps. Every thought of you, driving by places where we go to, used to. I know I blew out your moon."

"My gracious moon. My sun. You dimmed me. My world. Rewrote my entire universe."

"I know," they leaned closer. "I know. I left you in the dark, and it you became." They dip their head.

"I was in the twilight, broken, bruised, half dead-half alive, feeling used. I cried and cried, screeching. Cursing you as I sweet talked," I tell them.

"We were born to die. I lost myself; I won't lie. Many times, I made you cry," they gently caressed my chin with their soft fingers.

"I loved you, Algea. I loved you," I say, my voice quivering as a tear streams down my face.

"I know you did. I know you did. The poetry, the letter," they reach into a pocket. They take a folded piece of paper, unfolding it, and grinning. "I know you loved me. And I never told you then, but I loved you too. Whatever that was. Whatever we had."

"It's been almost eight years, darling Algea."

"That it has, that it has," they respond. "The misuse, the abuse. I didn't know if you'd even have me."

"This has been coming," I sipped again, drying my tears on a blue napkin. "Needed. My garden needed to be weeded. Your seeds have been persistent and invasive. Far too overgrown and persuasive."

"What I did was wrong. It was a sorrowful, waste-of-stardust type of song. You deserved better. I could never, did never, write you such a letter," Algea holds mine up. "I am sorry." I turn and look away, back towards Desire.

"Please look at me." I slowly turned back around to see their eyes. "I was clueless, inexperienced. I hurt you deeply. I am sorry."

"It's been rough. Your leaving was tough. It sunk in for me that day. The loss of you sunk in. Crept through," I replied.

"The Blue Neighborhood, in every shade of precious blue, will always remind me of you." Algea sighs. "I didn't come here to upset you or make you sad. This was the only method, the only way I had."

"I appreciate the apology, truly." My eyes followed their face lines and their hair as my face softened. "I appreciate the time and all you did for me. Especially opening me up."

"You did the same for me, so it is mutual," Algea smiles. "I'll let you go," they chuckle, making me chuckle too.

"Your pretty little lady over there is smiling up a storm," Algea nods to Desire.

"I'm no longer a post-storm poppy," I replied.

"Exactly," Algea says as they stand.

"You deserve peace and happiness. Things I never really properly gave you. Please, please do not let me stop you. Don't let me be the reason you aren't able to love again. You can love others and yourself again."

Algea rests a hand on my shoulder. "You can let me go, probably already have by now. We both know. So, go! Grow, flourish, bloom! Unravel me completely this time from your loom."

We stared at each other for a few seconds, minutes, maybe an hour, I wasn't sure. Tears in our eyes and down my cheek. "Take care," Algea finally hugged me hard. I did the same back, for once not feeling a heartless lack. Algea finished the neat, pushed up the chair seat, and, like that, watched their footsteps make an outward beat. As they walked out the doors, Monaxia swirled to the table to begin cleaning up. I had my hand clenched, and I reopened it slowly; this time, there was no bloody wound.

Instead, I found held within the first piece of my heart.

~talking with your ghost

the day will come
where the past is a faint hum
iridescent butterflies
bright from the sun
carry you to me
we meet in that meadow
and i move closer
filled by your light
~love me like you should

for a brief moment in the beginning
as we laid out on that blanket
i wrapped in your gray hoodie
arms around me
the flames will dance high
igniting hidden parts of me
~never out of style

love songs playing
cupid's chords blaring
as we dance in the living room
the whole world spinning for us
lost in the night
lost in each other
~you replay

the morning will dawn
the sun will rise
a fresh horizon
after my heart locked up
and everyone else
had the wrong
combination
~situation beneficial

With each hue, memory awakens, and soft blues tell of quiet days where, in gentle waves, trust conveys. Emerald greens in laughter shared, when held within each other's arms, souls are bared. Shades of violet speak of dreams in starlit skies the future gleams. Silvery strokes of moonlit nights, where in each other's gaze, they find their lights

Upon this canvas, with love as their guide, they paint side by side. A masterpiece of deep feelings. A gallery of hearts, forever to keep. Love is an art, tender and bold. A story in colors waiting to be told. Upon the canvas of love with each brushstroke, an unspoken oath. Love, the artist, bends at will.

~canvas of love

DIVINITY

lovesick
can't fight anymore
starlight
fire
sunlight
where are you
~not enough speed

the future is sweet
healing is bright
i am divine
i am heavenly
~divine

do as you desire
be careful of that high wire
love is quite strange
as it just begins
~grip on my mind

i know these trials and tribulations
these equations
bring me closer to see
to find healing and clarity
to bring me back
back to me
~return to me

i became trapped
trapped in pandora's
box
trapped within myself
denial
ignorance
affliction
~only lock and no key

i sold myself on fantasy
you
true blue garden pansy
it all felt so real
until through our layers
did i peel
~i see now

i finally learned
after a while
after trials
when it was hostile
there was no use in sitting
in betting
wondering why
if i didn't know then
i know now
~nm

that somebody is out there
stars twinkling in their hair
beauty so captivating you can only stare
and they'll make sense of what you called a mess
smiles
instead of cries
~searching aurora borealis

life changes fast
you can't replace
don't replace
what's stuck in the past
people we meet fade away
those of genuine or lessons
will stay
~present truth

you don't always know where to go
when the spark won't flame
you're on the ground
covered in splinters
surrounded by negative sprinters
scars from your past
unless you choose
the pain won't last
~leave wounds to heal

nothing is entirely certain
sometimes it is chess
sometimes it is a game
opening my eyes to the future
the blue lilies continue to bloom
and i can hear you saying my name
~voice of the future

perfect oceans
i couldn't breathe
held down like an anchor
until you
the new
weightlessness recedes
~scales rebalance

the past
the future
an unforgotten
but ignored
present
in open arms
through death
~hold me verthandi

id rather be alone
cold as stone
than let someone hold me
who doesn't mean it
unless they show me
~give me proof

lift
lift me out
lift
lift me out
lift me from doubt
lift
lift me from damaged skin
lift
lift me to your heavens
lift
lift me into your arms
lift
lift me to home again
~lift

i see you for a
house
a home
full of love
well being
~new feeling

ive waited for you
paralyzed
by my own will
by my own choices
as i'm reminded
viciously
the past was a crashing course
a boat steered by divine force
so now
in this moment
this present
you can be mine
and i
yours
~someone new, anew

we balance elements
fire and earth
water and air
reaching forth
with colors so vivid
that i wasted all these
years
eternity
finally
brought us here
~brought us to an end

at some point
through divine anoint
i will be swallowed
by the mouth of infinity
all of me
finally a divine trinity
where i smile through agony
bearing the weight of our existence
bearing the weight
of us
us two
~reunion with me, soon

once fell on my knees playing lost
no one heard what i was saying
only the skies above
as i saw pieces torn off
my soul flying
it was cause i was in an empty bed
no shoulder upon to rest my head
paralyzed legs
no one chasing me
as i rewrote my blank paper road
~the need of two

many a time
when we were together
when we were apart
the devil called my name
tempted me like eve
coiled around my sleeve
slithering to drink our pain
spill the holy water
sip and pour the poison
heavy vapors
no control over the words i say
so i wrote them
pen met paper
ink met essence
and i created
~letters for chasing shadows

the first few weren't heaven sent
more so hell bent
yet of divine descent
saved myself from original sin
a chorus of angels
healing sings
~lessons, not sins

Blanche lived in the past. She embodied it. She was rehashing old mistakes. There are no solid grounding brakes. Just deep, heartfelt quakes. Perceived mistakes soured with regret. Her obsession was Belle Reve. Mine, the heart I wear on my sleeve. The push pins to my doll jabbing the future. I rip those out because I have control over the sutures. I have control over my life. I can change or set my future.
~divinity

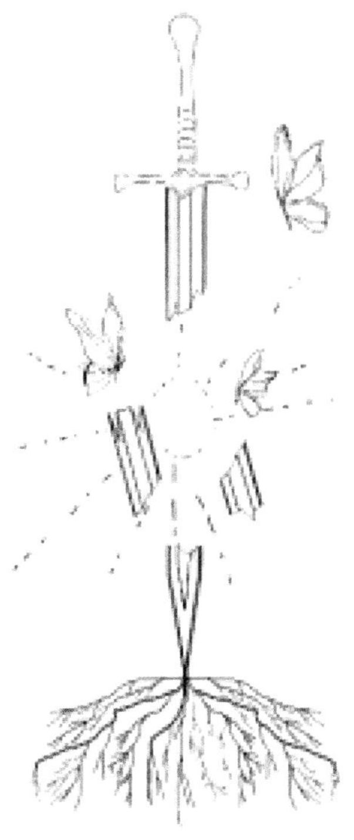

INTERNAL ALCHEMY

back to eden
no one told me to breathe
crystal waters
pathways higher
patient violence
bury that history
rewrite the telomeres
~who said love was easy

one day
your love will come into me
i'll feel it slow
reality over a dream
touching me with a kiss
touching me
honestly
~all for you

moving on is the way to go
heal, reflect, know
it feels like a one way road
a jagged path long and dark
but that is where a seed starts
~road of potential

i was living in a war zone
fields of bloody poppies
heart full of bullet holes
boarded up windows
riding out a past storm
broken petals all in that war zone
~the great war

victim of a chemical cut
a heartache rut
yet this is scary
this chemical rebalance
i can get down with peaceful silence
you highlight me like the moon
let me out like hounds
a dangerous unknown disposition
to be so free
to be refracted in light
reflected
in the sound of your voice
~hold me in daylight

oh again
as you smirk and grin
i can tell i'm falling
falling further and further again
this time though
i won't turn away
~feet planted firmly

we don't know what we got
until its lost
when we lose it
it won't stick around
if we don't choose it
~dance with a stranger

when that fateful day comes
i will be scared
i will be a pile of nerves
insecure about my curves
and knowing while i've been healing
left inside this chest
is a still a broken heart piece
and when you ask for it
to hold and cherish
i will be afraid
i should've been more careful
~hold what i am

you'll make me feel
you'll make it more
it'll be more than ever before
it'll be more to feel
than before
~how to feel

A crash echoes. An old shell. Withering shadow. A ghost that reaches for your glass jar. Half burnt ashes. Tears collected upon my lashes. To restore its power was its solemn goal.

"No!" I cried out, grabbing its bag of knives and swords.

I zipped its venomous mouth as it writhed.

"I will not drown," I said. "I will not drown in them again."

~internal alchemy

PHOENIX

it's beautiful
this lie i lived
but time is over
that old way is on it's way out
no more
of the dark paradise
~even candles light the dark

this is where i wanna be
happy
with you
in my gray hoodie
~saw once on screen

when i thought the world of you
that was it
you were the world
the galaxy
now i see you
you were just a spec of dust
in my universe
~dream in the dark

it's funny how its different
our hands on different bodies
our minds on different hobbies
and i am now growing
a new field of poppies
after poppy hypnosis

everybody was asking
what happened
i changed
as we're supposed to
~metamorphosis

they'll treat me right
put me first
hold their word
fight for love
hold on tight
not go extinct like a passenger dove
~good one

we know out there
in the vastness
the stars will align
it's already been written
when we give our heart away
lay it all on the line
you'll actually mean it
this time
~future delivery

something else may one day burn
from the past's overturned urn
a little too fast
that burn
because i'll be in disbelief
someone can be this good
~what is out there

i'm free as a bird
no string ties
wings unbound
i fly high
cause they're gone
~cage is open

i don't know you
not yet at least
yet somehow i do
i've seen you
parts of you
so i will wait
to meet you
~please come down out of that tree

as the night seeps in
the fireflies dance
the crickets sing
we dance slow
beneath their glow
bare feet
dirt road
~trust in you

i'm scared
i don't know to start
what if a little love
tears us apart
~scared of this heart

trying to live it up
only to break down
taking you back up
but ive turned the page
learning to trust again
waiting for someone
my starlight
my burning sun
~hero's journey

just like a gentle rain
you cast away the dust
repolished the rust
wash the salt out my hands
freshwater eyes
dissolving the fears
scares
and shadows
~no more rust

i know
i know
stoic cycle over
get what you give
recap what is sown
but i can see you
i see you in my fate
~will you saturate

after being stuck for so long
counted my rights
denied my wrongs
i laid my anchor
in a different harbor
non-choppy waters
~not holding on

when the day comes
those nights
i lay awake
you drifting through my mind
and i'm waiting
for your love
~patience

i already feel it
the peace you bring me
the rarity i felt i never find
contrast to the chaos of solitude devices
you took my heart
without sacrifices
~new heart power

i light the fire
in the cold wilderness
you are the nourishing warmth
the flames
you are the light
that within and ignited
i hope you'll love me forever
you hope i return soon
you take away the pain
you are the start of a new everything
~from ashes come anew

i can see the future sense
feel the psychic sense
when you love me
see me for me
how will it first be
cause my heart will bleed
i won't be able to breathe
ill recluse to be alone
so please
don't put down your phone
~give me what i need

I raced through the blue neighborhood. A pace you set. Frantic. Panic is a false enchantment. Time has changed so much. And after running through ages, I'm erasing your pages. It was you, just you, through my false perception, that made it the blue neighborhood.

~Phoenix

There I stood in a grand hall. Long as it was tall. Infinite, no real definite.

"The Hall of the Present," a feminine voice echoes out. The snowy white rippled image appears in the darkness, contrasting the great starkness. She hugs me as the sweet scent of jasmine fills my head. Her white gown rustles in the breeze, adorned with a flower crown, holding a bright bouquet of three dark-centered, canary yellow sunflowers.

"This where I ended up, back to your authority," I say, taking one of the flowers she handed me.

"That is quite so," her nose wiggles as she laughs. "You do know the why."

"That I do." I smell the flower as a familiar box appears upon a small marble table, lit by a single sun ray.

"It's your box," her hand motions to it. I took the notion and walked up to it. It sprawled out a long pink tongue, like bubblegum. A single large eye sat atop the darkness of the void as it fully opened. It's slit pupil looked down, down at the tongue tip. Here laid a photograph, a past Polaroid. Written on the back, as I held it, was "VOID". It was a photograph of You and I, of Unraveling of Us.

"I only vaguely remember this day," I say. "It's been so long ago."

"Time has shuffled a lot," she says. A continuous go, nonstop."

"A happy moment," I hold it up. "That sparkle in my eyes, a moment where I'm not shy. Yet the very person that always made me cry."

"You've spoken to my sister. Your past lies here and there in her pool, where she's been leaving it. Tending it to move you forward."

"This meeting with you," I look at her.

She smiles to me. "I am a collection of The Past with well. Present concepts and decisions based upon time before. And whether you settle the score or not. So, if not, that is when the last becomes the present."

She holds up her measuring rod. "As you work, if that is the decision, my sister and I wade. Into the waters, clearing the debris. Clearing that which no longer serves, ushering in what you deserve."

"Muck removal," I grin, as does she.

"Water lilies blossom, lotus too," she caresses the sunflower blossoms in her hand, "bud through the mud. To reach the top. To bloom with the bright light of day."

"You speak truth and have been honest with yourself, the most potent healing. Patchwork improvement from demon dealing. That wretched poker game, hearts, and minds sold are nowadays of old. And so, while you're being bold..." she points her rod to the box.

"A cheer," I hold up the Polaroid to what was perfect imperfection. "A good lesson, the advice," I rub the photo with my thumb. "The self-love you gave me, the truths, the growths, a lasting impression. Right and wrong direction, once again, perfect imperfection."

I move closer to the box. "So, my dear box, ignite." A deep growl echoed from it, tongue flickering, hickory dickering as Phoenix feathers sport out. Molten flames caught fire within the darkness of its void, and its tongue turned to magma with a black lava top.

"I take this sweet confection, past concoction, crossed star decoction, and relieve its duties." I place the Polaroid onto the lava-crusted tongue, which slurps it into the fiery void. "Burn like the rains!"

I set fire to the rain. I could hear it screaming out One last time, in a doppelgänger voice like my own, as the photo caught fire, knowing I'd thrown us into the fire. I watched the water pour as it burnt and my box burped a spray of ash.

"Here is to goodbye," I wipe my lash. The tongue retracts and the lid slams shut.

~the burning of us

She was the youngest, with no wrinkles and only smooth crinkles. Her smile yielded soft dimples.

"I am the evolution of Past and Present, a mirror if one will. I am determined by processing what was before and what is now. I am detailed yet broad. I am the sacred union of before and now."

"The future's composition, based upon the previous decomposition," I breathe. "You are The After," I smile.

"Correct, you are, dearest one," she rubs my shoulder with her strong, pale hands. "You have one last guest, as time is fleeting. You are in the process of a powerful healing. The Wheel is sleeting."

"One last guest, or so permanent resident," I add as it steps from the shadows. Shrouded it was, for it knew no gender. It was natural, yet also a pretender. A collection of galactic fabrics overlaid and folded for a loose shape. A white-masked face, red lips, and many splintery hands. Some were barren, some were human, some were flawed. Some were long-nailed, some looking as if straight from Hell. Dozens more hovered around it, unattached, bearing small blue flames.

Memoria looks at me as I approach it, bowing. It bows back, even though it only floated. As it does

"You know me, it seems," the hands sqwirm as their long nails gleam.

"You are Chandoo, The Night's Reach. All-encompassing, dreams or nightmares, glances or stares, closeness or care, even rabbit or bear." I hold out a hand as it wrinkles its lips. Its main large hand, cold yet warm, grips mine, as we shake, as the hovering hands shake my other. "You are the fabric of my reality. You are Paranoia. You are whatever I make you."

I turn and look to Memoria, then to After. "At the slightest event of heartbreak, of that wretched tearing and ache, the mind loses composition. Begins its descent into decomposition."

"Exactly," she smiles. "So, with that said, before you get too into your head, I am sending you on a trip. Snow boots are wise; please don't trip. Chandoo often joins Her. You know her well. So, off you go, be swell."

I blink, and suddenly, I have been transported, transmuted. It is a cold evening, spitting snow and pellets of ice pummeling. I looked and wandered onward, wherever I was. My movement was not fast, but also not slow. I was warm, wrapped in an ancient pelt gifted to me by Beira, Bear Lady of Frost.

Running beside me, feet crunching in fresh snow, was White Paw. His coat was soft; he was perfectly white. A water-loving white wolf totem. He trotted joyfully alongside me as we neared a large meadow encompassed by eternal spring. Bluebells, foxgloves, daffodils, and herbs are all sprinkled in this small paradise, free of snow-like stripes. Seated in the middle, chimney smoking, was a well-lit hut.

I shed the pelt, setting it on the skull-decorated gates, which many hated. The birch tree waved as the gate opened, and White Paw remained beside me. Birch was a gentle tree, and it pushed forward me. I stopped as the hut door opened, revealing an elderly grandmother adorned in colorful Slavic fabric.

"Grandson!" her strong, accented voice rang out, knocking snow off the trees and sending warm shivers through me. "Join us!"

A warm presence, her hut. So welcoming, so gentle, as I stepped inside, and White Paw beside me, she motioned to a large wooden table, pre-set. I sit, white fur beneath me like man's best friend.

"Emotions are a powerful thing. They are human nature. But it can make or break, causing a ruckus. Even if nothing is at stake."

"Part of the waking world," I tell her as she sets down a bowl filled with fragrant herbal chicken stew, all she prepared and grew. She sat down another wooden bowl of beef broth, topped with rosemary and thyme.

"I used to handle them somewhat better until the hiccups of the last few years."

"Those years were out of your hands. You weren't in control of any of Time's great sands," she says, pouring me more tea. "What was it you were told?"

"Bent, not broken," I respond.

"Precisely," she hands me a silver spoon and sits across from me, grabbing a more miniature marble mortar and pestle.

As I eat, my eyes take in the room, lit by luscious candles: bee and animal wax dipped in herbs. Hag tapers, falsely named, alighted the dinner table, simply mullein wrapped in beeswax.

They flickered softly, little imps dancing, a fire jig. The candle jitterbugs. Upon a soft bear skin rug.

Tall wooden shelves, a row of tea and coffee mugs crafted from precious clay. Books upon books, many ancient by their looks. Volumes of forgotten lore amongst bundles of fabrics, dyed yarn, crafted cloth. All were bright and pastel colors, patterned and plain. Some even had the essence of rain. Bundles of herbs, fresh and dried, hung and gently swung from the rafters. Animal skulls, antique human skulls, and artifacts decoratively littered around, and a sweeping broom automatically swept the ground.

A loom-like and wood- stood in the corner behind where she sat. Glowing white thread and golden wads sat on the floor and wrapped on the loom. I swallow and motion my head towards it. She grins, reaching up to grab bouquets of herbs. "Your loom, Baboushka, looks very old. All the fabrics it must have helped hold."

"The Time it has helped mold," she tells me. It is a predecessor, bones of things before your time. Threads of destiny mixed with those of time. Cosmic blankets, magical items, and trinkets." She tosses in pinches, herbal dashes, as she mashes with the pestle.

I grab some bread as she continues to speak.

Emotions are valuable; they make you human, even as pestering as they are. At times, they feel like you have been hit by a car. Yet, you don't want to be numb."

"I used to think that." She nods, knowing it already to be true. "But not anymore really. It was just silly."

"An understandable desire," she replies. "You are, though, created with very intricate wire. I have seen emotions hurt, flirt, burn, help. It is all up to you. They are your emotions, after all. Sometimes, you don't hold control, but you generally do. You can construct what they will affect and how much power they carry.

whether you'll be grim or merry." Her soft eyes look up at me while she grinds. "You've chosen to carry yours without influence or sherry."

"A curse most tell me," I roll my eyes.

"But it shows your strength, character, and understanding of the world, as my Sister has told you."

"There's power in emotion," I tell her. "In identity. But it can be a cure or a toxic potion. So, how, how Babushka, does one learn control?"

"That secret lies within you. It's trial and error, looking at yourself and things in the mirror. Understanding emotions value. Why do you have them? What they do. Feel them, don't shoo. Dig down and find the root; it might be a goldenseal or a screeching mandrake root. Those that serve you well keep and grow to be swell. Those that do not that banshee root give them the boot. But do not feel that is the biggest mistake you or humanity have made. Not feeling and recognizing the emotions, hiding them, creates a most toxic sludge film."

She grabs a few more herbs and dried flowers, mixing a secret potion with her antique power. "You should sit with them, hear them out. From a place of understanding and balance, your Libran forte. Sit and listen to what they have to say. Honor their existence, but don't give any of them too much persistence. Emotions get the best of you. The red one, especially

"Anger," I sigh.

"It is a wicked emotion, but you inherited it, and it doesn't have to be like that. Like he was and is. It's your decision how it plays out and how you use it. Shutting down that generational trauma and healing it. Also, take a couple of candles with your grandson when you leave a scrap of my fabric: the Feya, The

Vila, and Vilenjak, and I weave. Feathers from Zhar-Ptista to help light your way.

A sweeping of fabric echoes as the white-gowned figure Urdlorumr enters the room. She turns to me, a gentle smile stretching across her eternal face.

"You burnt fear, those past you's have been settled. You are on a new bike so to speak, a much better peddle". She reaches into her robes, taking out a shiny stone tablet embedded with precious gems. "This is a stone mirror. Your ancestors used it-divination, scrying -when you need inner reflection." I take it from her. Use it, as it can show you any part of yourself."

Another rustling, fabric jostling, brings an older twin. Babushka's sister, yesteryear twister. "An arrowhead from your tribe," Beira opens my hand, her rough, solid skin brushing my palm as she places it inside, closing it. Her open arms, adorned in drabs of bear skin and dark-colored woolen cloth, wrap me in a polar hug, which I return.

Babushka strides towards me, kissing my forehead. I encase her in a hug, and she returns it, rubbing my back. Letting go, I head for the open door, items, candles, feathers, all in hand. Stopping, I turned around, and see her still staring at me still, mouth cracked open. "I am proud of you. What you've accomplished."

Urdlorumr looks at me. "Learnt and grown, new seeds sown," she says.

Tears swell in my eyes as some grace my cheeks. "I appreciate you all." They nod. "Thank you, Urdlorumr." She smiles, the most in a while, then turns back around.

~black forest babushka

In all my lonely nights, I'm afraid. A toxic persuade. Scared of the future, haunted by the past. That which taints my perception.

"Where are we walking to?" Memoria asks me as we turn the corner.

"I am not sure M," I respond. "We are just going to be going. Walking is solace, as best as the power of the feet can withhold."

"I see, Sir, let us walk."

There was a darkness, a starkness, that was covering my lands. My entire universe. It was an entity, a repre-sentity of all that was hidden. All that was forbidden. It was all-encompassing and yet a crucial aspect of everything. It resided within, typically, more so formally, the Dark Lands where my shadows were held. Yet, it, they, was here as the orb that had been following us morphed into a figure. "Hello, Darkness, or Nyxaria, I should say."

"Both are synonymous, Sir. Call me, call us, what you wish".

"You are usually my shadows, my bad lows. Rare is it to have you out in the day," I say, taking its coal-colored hand.

"You know why I am here, sir?" It takes my hand.

"Your rebirth is most exquisite. Your buds are ready to bloom when the time comes right," Memoria states.

"It is taking a toll," my head dips. "Hence why I am wandering here, going for a stroll."

"To be reborn, one must crumble. It will shake you to the core and cause quite the stir and rumble", Nyxaria states, hovering around me as we continue to walk.

"Is your brother-sister at The Fields?" I ask it, following like a shadow stalking.

"Quite so, it is so. Run, arrowhead throw."

~pathway to the fields

"So desolate, so undaunted," I said, peering around. I was drinking from stained glass, seated under a makeshift tent on a patch of bullet-hole-riddled grass. The field I was in was also riddled and fiddled with bomb craters and empty cannons- all war-based shenanigans. Tall, red, solid poppies lined the deepest craters, bleeding the deep wounds and cradling the injuries of the landscape. Soft purple poppies, from white to lavender and other pastels, blanketed the rest of the field. There was little between still young green rosettes of growing poppies, those in full blossom or buds about to bloom, and purely barren land like a lava flow. It was a solemn, somniferous show.

Memoria stood at my side, my war general. Nyxaria had gone back to their darkness-filled corners in my Plane. As I drank, my lips purple-hued from sipping poisoned wine by my hand, and I scanned the scarred land.

"It is coming," Memoria draws closer to me, hands folded behind her back.

"It is already here," I point to the foggy edges of the darkened forests surrounding my fields. Faint blue orbs were circling and floating. A loud crack caused us both to look upwards like Old Mother Hubbard cleaning her cupboards. A time warp, a crack-like sliver highlighted in bright silver, opened in the partially blue sky midway of the field.

"You're bleeding out," she told me, rubbing my shoulder. My focus shifted from watching the blue orbs sail to the center field, with coal-black mist pouring in from the sliver above. "You have colored all the boulders behind you. The road you came here on."

I turned and looked with a great sigh and felt as if I had brought a cursed book. Crimson stains littered the ground and pathway, as well as drops of blood as well. It was as if a holy cardinal laid down his robe or a cartographer shattered his most perfect globe.

My other guest stepped forward from the tent's corners, sipping a glass of pink champagne. Her translucent pink toile was magnificent, never lame. "It is the past," Desire says. "Writhing from your crypt, from the rediscovered tombs by your rebirth. As the digging progresses, The Past is no longer serving pain and stress. Compresses and regresses."

"I would rather it not," I respond. "It is painful. I want it out of me, just not like I'm being battered with a million red hot poker bees".

"But," she caresses my shoulder, "you are the bees' knees." Her poppy red lips form a crescent moon smile as I take her hand.

"It's an ongoing fight." I pluck a poppy blossom, watching white sap slither down its pale blue stem. I crumple, rumple, the blossom in my hand. "Mainly, staining because this field and all of mine are full of the poppies I adore. Poppies of the Past."

"Paranoia Poppies," a rasping wail calls out. We all look up, and hovering before us is the shrouded, coal-clouded figure of Chandoo. It had changed capes, now bearing a landscape wardrobe covered in thousands of eyes, like the thousand injuries of Fortunato. Three masks in white, unholy shades of what was a mock to Heavenly light, hung around its neck, with two more on its horns.

"Well, the mask brigade has arrived," I sit my glass down. "Another detonation, and I may not survive."

"You know what you seek, sir." Memoria pats my shoulder, helping me refocus. "What we seek."

"Peace."

"I hate to set these fields on fire," I take her hand as Desire rests her hand on my other shoulder, my guardian sentinels. "Yet, it is much needed. All their beauty and growth has only been for me to choke."

"Fire rejuvenation is much needed," Desire says, taking a drink. "These are, as said, Paranoia Poppies. Their centers look astounding, but they pollinate with grains of deception. They are toxic recollections.

"They are foul-seeded," Memoria tightens her grip. "They must be weeded."

"Even these poppies, with numbing innocence colored sap, destroy your mind with a rotten, buzzing zap. Captivating beauty," Desire motions, "of fantasies and falsehoods."

"Drinking wine infused with monkshood." I see the two women nod. I stand up, brushing myself off and seeing the red stain in the chair and the puddle around it. I could feel myself, out there in 3D, shaking as the candle began to flicker.

"How much backlash are you going to give me?" I turn to Chandoo.

"Let this be a peace treaty," Chandoo's main face looks at me.

"A peace treaty from Paranoia? This feels like a setup."

Memoria steps forward. "Look within, look and feel what your 3D self is. The candle is burning; every part of you is yearning."

Chandoo holds out its main hand. I walk up to its floating presence, all its eyes and pupils staring directly at me. "This is our peace treaty, here in The Fields of.

"Soon to be renamed," Desire holds up her glass in a cheer.

"As witnessed by Trust, me, and Desire." My hand meets that of Chandoo, where the dozens of eyes upon its arm and shoulder blink rapidly. I let go of its hand, looking at my palm. A tattoo, black inked with purple, painted its center. It was a single, carefully detailed eye. Flipping over, the back of my hand was a line drawing of poppy petals, even down to my fingers.

"These are our markings," Chandoo caresses the tattoos with its long nails. "This is evidence of not only our agreement, but healing, positive dealing."

"Let these tattoos empower you," Desire takes my hand. "Let the guide you, just like Dorothy's red shoe."

My head twitches, glitches. Memoria smiles, and Desire is back behind me, taking her hand. "It is time," my lips quiver as I move forward to a large crater with bloody, splotched, pink-flowered poppies. Their stems twist and turn, sloppy. Two open flowers move their heads to my gaze, and for the first time, I see their centers are glaring eyes. Piercing me with their deceptive lies.

3D begins to recite, and I recite a poem, holding up the new tattooed hand.

"In the twilight's amber glow, where poppies gently sway, I sing, I recite, to release what my heart holds at bay. Embers dance upon the breeze, secrets in the fiery tide- and the field of scarlet dreams, where emotions cannot hide." The tattoo on my hand began to glow bright golden light

This is the chorus of the burning bloom, petals aflame at night."

Memoria approaches me, gently grabbing my elbow as I turn around. She handed me a wooden torch, an early ancestral skull at its end. The black eye sockets were like soul-tingling rockets. My tattooed hand takes it, making me get goosebumps. And in my throat were many lumps. This was a torch meant to scorch.

"Gentle zephyrs carry tales on the tongues of the pyre. A symphony of crackling flames, a dance of wild desire."

"I want to say I'm sorry, but that is the past," I look to Chandoo.

"I too wish to be healed, Sir," Chandoo hovers to a reasonable distance before me. "I am a remnant from the human past. Sabretooth, bears, wretched betrayal like Macbeth."

"Macbeth! Macbeth!" whispers from within Chandoo echoed back.

I held up my palm, the eye blinking rapidly. It locked onto Chandoo. "I am sorry, Chandoo, for what I have done to us." Its mouth formed a soft smile as a tear dropped down my face, falling like feathers and lace. "There are no morning glories, not this time. This was many battles, many bloody, bloody wars."

I kept reciting. "In each flicker, let go the sorrow, the woes of past and tomorrow, let it drift away,

as poppies turn to ashes, with the dying of the day." The torch quivers in my hand as the eye sockets shiver. Quickly, they turned bright with yellow, healing but destructive mellow, as they ignited. They faced our tent, but it was time I repented. I nodded to Chandoo and turned the skull toward the field. The poppies were screaming in whispers, deception, recollection, screaming Your and Your name, all held within an unraveling of us.

"Crimson whispers on the wind, fiery song, burn these fields of poppies, where emotions don't belong." The skull squeals as streams, molten beams, sail out of the sockets and cracked mouth. They slam into the fields, screeching, beseeching, as they took root and began to spread.

My focus turned to Chandoo's central head. "Let the flames be your confessor, as they flicker, twist, and twine, in these poppies of yours and mine," it chanted. "The pyre of poppy fields, may your emotions unwind, no longer be intertwined."

We both spoke at the same time, a long-needed shared rhyme. "Release the held emotions in a burning poppy pyre." A second ricochet of flames charges out of the skull with golden threads from the tattoo as if they were a comet's tail. It was Chandoo, their target, that they did rail. It was hit like one of Helena's nails, sending Chandoo into an explosion of blue, green, and yellow flames. The soundwaves, filled with relief and implosion, rippled out. They collided with me as I closed my tear-filled eyes, my eyelids lit by the glow of the fire I had started; I had sat. I was burning the karmic debt. I was burning the previous start. I was revitalizing injured and shattered parts. My whole body quivered, and I shook, falling back, opening my eyes to see Memoria's hands had caught me reading many books.

After a few moments, Memoria props me back up, taking the skull torch. The tattoo was still on my hand, and it stung, but all of me stung, a ringing out within me that just rang.

"As the ashes settle softly on the ground once filled with pink, purple, white, and red," I say, wiping my eyes and looking around.

"Feel the weight lift from your heart, as if a curse has been shed," Memoria and Desire say in unison.

The fields were now purely barren; there was no more poppy sharing. The soil was scorched, and the chunks and blocks of rock, too. A blanket of soft false volcanic ash covered the ground; it was quiet, a first snow kind of sound. Like the batting of lashes, Ashes fluttered around still in the smoky air. Many had landed in my hair.

"Once blossom-filled fields are now a wasteland."

"Hope is not lost, Mr. Gatsby," Chandoo's voice echoes out from the implosion-looking mark a few feet away from me. The scorch marks leaked darkness as it and ash pulled together, forming Chandoo's familiar figure. Yet, this time, it was more so a disfigure. There was less fabric, less shroud, more of a humanoid hunched figure, still in coal and grey sky-colored garb. Blue flaming hands materialized as the more petite, white-faced mask met my gaze. There were still eyes dotting this slimmer body, but they were far fewer. A few dozen, not the previous thousands to millions. I was etched in relief, for once not feeling the stares of trillions.

I walked to Chandoo, ash covering my bare feet and making small drifts. My poppy sketched hand met its large, long, nailed main hand. Our palms were united, my tattoo glowing brilliantly as we let go. My hand moved to the masks still hanging off its horns and as a necklace.

"We must burn these masks, yet not right now," Chandoo tells me. "You know what they are already."

"That I do," my fingers run along a couple.

"You should plant the feathers," another whisper from Chandoo's fabrics called out. I turned to Memoria as she tossed me the sparkling tail feathers of Zhar-Ptitsa. She held onto one, but I had the other eight. Each was long, like a falcon mixed with a peacock, some bent, others perfectly straight. My still weak knees bent down, moving back ash. My fingers turned red-clay black as I dug into the now-soft soil. I buried the feathers and covered them up. Beneath the soil, they were brightly emitting red, orange, and yellow light, like a bonfire set at twilight.

Chandoo hovered over me and handed me a small envelope. It was a seed packet wrapped in a loving full-color jacket. *Elysian Fields Seed Company* in bright white stamped at the top. A heart-shaped outline was filled with an image of poppies, zinnias, cosmos, calendula, sunflowers, coneflower, bee balm, and phlox.

I tore the top of the packet, knowing it was enchanted. I poured the seeds into my palm and then handed it off to Memoria and Desire, where they did the same. We began making our way, sowing seeds as if to pray around the field. The seeds landed atop the ash as Desire, me, and Memoria met in the center, realizing our pathway made a perfectly shaped heart.

"Reminders of days bright and gray," I turn and look across the field. "The sun sets low in a canvas sky,

Painting hues of goodbye with beams of golden dye. Fear not the twilight, the stars will guide, through the memory garden, side by side. In this sanctuary, where moments reside, Love is the *gardener, side by side. Tending to blossoms, both young and old, in this garden, where stories are told."*

~cutting cords

The End

ABOUT THE AUTHOR

Stephen Smith is an avid gardener of Guthrie, Kentucky with extensive experience in plant breeding and genetics and seed saving. He holds a bachelors degree in Agriculture from Austin Peay State University and holds a Masters of Teaching in Secondary English from the University of the Cumberlands. Stephen is passionate about heirloom seeds, literature, environmental stewardship, botany, conservation, sustainability. His writing features the genres of poetry, young adult fiction, supernatural fiction, and nonfiction.

OTHER WORKS

Stephen Smith

The Unraveling of Us

"There's darkness in the distance. A painful, aggravated experience. Love is its foundation, loss is it's firefly fuel. Wound up on Fate's spool is healing and its accomplishments when done. A new Dawn is born, as the heart reopens bound in vibrant rose petals, inviting you to fall in." Stephen Smith

Blurb: It's been years since your expulsion from what was once Us. I still feel the spin. You never left my mind, body, and heart. It hurts to remember, and I feel those things I never wanted to feel again. There's not much I can do anymore but hold my breath and try to push you out of my chest. You were love. You were home. Now I am once again alone.

Semper Augustus

Reece Archer, the contemplative owner of Elysian Fields flower shop, has always found joy and solace among the fragrant blooms and in the pages of his journals, where he crafts stories from the quiet comfort of his botanical haven. Romance was never a priority—until a spontaneous journey to the tulip-filled landscapes of Holland introduces him to Dylan Prescott. Charismatic and brimming with life, Dylan is a star athlete whose sincerity and zeal ignite an unexpected spark in Reece, revealing a connection that feels both profound and inevitable.

Though they discover the astonishing fact that they have been neighbors in Streetcar Junction for years, it is only among the vibrant fields of Holland that their paths are destined to cross. As Reece and Dylan explore the serendipitous threads of their connection—amidst the vivid backdrop of tulips, the bustling football scenes at Streetcar University, and the petal-strewn paths of Reece's shop—they are compelled to consider the possibilities of a future together. Their story is a testament to the unpredictable rhythms of love, urging them to embrace the dance of destiny that has drawn them together against all odds.

Made in the USA
Columbia, SC
21 November 2024